Ollie's
Magic Bunny

D1103587

90710 000 387 778

Ollie and her toy bunny had been
waiting for the rain to stop for
a long, long time.

At last, that day had arrived! They rushed
to get ready – there were so many puddles
outside to splash in!

Ollie spotted the perfect puddle
straight away, but before she
could jump in . . .

Whooooosh!

A sudden breeze whistled past
bringing a cloud of blossom with it.

"Does that tickle, Bunny?" Ollie laughed.
A tiny petal had landed on his nose.

Bunny didn't answer, but
his nose began to twitch!

Ollie thought she must have
imagined it, but when she
looked again, his ears were
moving too.

Suddenly, Bunny sprang from the
basket towards a group of rabbits.

"Wait for me!" Ollie cried . . .

but they had already raced out of sight.

"Bunny?" called Ollie softly.

"Bunny! Where are you?"

Her voice grew louder and louder
as she searched and searched.

But she couldn't find him.

Ollie was so worried, she didn't notice the dark clouds gathering overhead.

Just as she was wondering if she would ever see Bunny again, Ollie spotted something . . . and gasped!

"Bunny, is that you?"

The water was rising and Bunny was in danger! But Ollie didn't know how to help.

Then she remembered her umbrella.

If only the magical breeze would blow again.
Ollie closed her eyes tightly and wished and wished . . .

Whooooosh!

She leaned out as far as she could,
reached for Bunny, and grabbed
him just in time.

"I'm so glad you're safe," she whispered.

But Bunny was very cold and they needed to find shelter.

Pitter patter,

pitter patter,

pitter patter.

When the rain finally stopped,
Ollie knew it was time to go home.
She just didn't know the way.

Maybe Bunny knew?

He raced higher and
higher up the tree . . .

until he reached the very top
and leapt onto a passing cloud!

What could Ollie do?

She took a deep breath,
opened her umbrella . . .

. . . and jumped too!

Ollie and Bunny floated through the sky, amazed by all the different clouds they could see, and how small everything looked below.

Then with a final

whooooosh...

the breeze brought them down towards home.

"Can you believe the adventure we've had, Bunny?" asked Ollie as they went inside. But he didn't answer.

Ollie looked down and blinked.

Bunny was a toy again!

It was getting late, but there was just time for Ollie to
read Bunny a story before bed. She carefully tucked
his petal inside the book to keep it safe.

"Night night, Bunny," Ollie whispered sleepily.

Bunny didn't reply. But as Ollie's eyes closed,
she was sure his nose was twitching . . .